Rainbow Days

The Gray Day

Written by
Valerie Bolling

Art by
Kai Robinson

ACORN™
SCHOLASTIC INC.

For my nieces, Anyah and Zorah, who provided the inspiration
for Zoya's character and her name. May all in your lives glitter!
—VB

To Jay
—KR

Text copyright © 2023 by Valerie Bolling
Illustrations copyright © 2023 by Kai Robinson

Library of Congress Cataloging-in-Publication Data

Names: Bolling, Valerie, author. | Robinson, Kai (Illustrator), illustrator.
Title: The gray day / written by Valerie Bolling ; illustrated by Kai Robinson.
Description: First edition. | New York : Acorn/Scholastic Inc., [2023] |
Series: Rainbow days ; 1 | Audience: Ages 4–6. | Audience: Grades K–1.
| Summary: On a rainy day, a young artist struggles to find
inspiration—until she remembers all the things she loves that are black and white.
Identifiers: LCCN 2021040589 (print) |
ISBN 9781338805932 (paperback) | ISBN 9781338805949 (library binding)
Subjects: LCSH: Painting—Juvenile fiction. | Colors—Juvenile fiction. |
Rain and rainfall—Juvenile fiction. | CYAC: Painting—Fiction. |
Color—Fiction. | Rain and rainfall—Fiction. | LCGFT: Fiction.
Classification: LCC PZ7.1.B656 Gr 2023 (print) |
DDC 813.6 [E]—dc23/eng/20220503
LC record available at https://lccn.loc.gov/2021040589

10 9 8 7 6 5 4 3 2 1   23 24 25 26 27

Printed in China   62
First edition, May 2023
Edited by Katie Carella
Book design by Jaime Lucero

Glitter

My name is Zoya.
I love to make art.

My puppy is my best friend.
His name is Coco. He makes art, too!

Today is the perfect day to paint.
I'll make my best painting yet!

Coco and I grab our art supplies.

I bring paper.

I bring paint and paintbrushes.

Coco brings the glitter.

I cannot wait to paint what I see!
I look at the leaves on the trees.

I see orange, red, and yellow.
There are spots of green, too.

I draw the trees. I fill in their colors with paint.

Coco adds a paw print that looks like a heart.

The sun shines through the leaves.
It makes the colors sparkle.

Oh! Oh! I know!
It's time for glitter.

Swoosh!

Now my leaves sparkle like the sun.

Uh-oh! Where did the sun go?
The sky fills with dark clouds.

Drip, drip. I hear rain on the steps.
Plop, plop. I feel rain on my arm.

My painting is getting wet!
The colors run into one another.

Glitter runs off the paper.

The wet grass sparkles.

Coco and I grab our art supplies.
We run inside!

Rain

I want to make a bright painting.
But all I see outside is gray.

I listen to the raindrops tap on my window.
I hear thunder.

The thunder sounds like a drum.
Boom, boom.

I don't want to paint the rainy sky.
What can I draw that's gray?

Oh! Oh! I know!
Gray is black and white!

I kiss Coco's black nose.

I rub his white belly.

Black is like the sky at night.
I like to see the moon smile at me.

I think of other things I like that are black.
My dress shoes. Teddy's button eyes.

Daddy's beard is black.

It tickles me when he gives me a kiss.

White is like the snow.
It's fun to make snow angels in my yard.

I think of other things I like that are white.
Fairy wings. Seashells at the beach.

Dandelions are white.

I blow them to make wishes.

Coco wags his tail on one painting.
It makes gray swirls. I like it.

My paintings need one more thing.
Swoosh! Glitter makes them sparkle!

Leaves

Today is a very gray day!
Even my paintings are gray. They need color.

The leaves on the trees are wet.
But they're colorful.

I will make my own leaves!
They will make my paintings colorful.

I grab my paper.

Coco gets my scissors.

I snap and snip. I cut and clip.

I cut leaves out of paper:

yellow,

orange,

red,

and green.

I glue them to my pictures.
My gray paintings are full of color!

I tape the bright paintings to my walls.
Now my walls are full of color.

I have one picture left.
Where will I hang it?

Oh! Oh! I know!
I want to cover the gray outside.

I tape the last picture to my window.
But then I see the sun!

Coco and I grab our art supplies.
We head outside!

I collect leaves and string them together.
Swoosh! Glitter makes everything better.

I put the necklace around Coco's neck.
I think he likes it!

Coco and I run and jump together.
We love all the bright colors we see!

About the Creators

Valerie Bolling has art on the walls of her home in Connecticut. But she's better at writing than painting. Her niece Zorah loves to write, too. Her niece Anyah loves making art projects like Zoya. Valerie is the author of LET'S DANCE!, TOGETHER WE RIDE, and RIDE, ROLL, RUN: TIME FOR FUN! Rainbow Days is her first early reader series.

Kai Robinson is an illustrator and designer based in New England. Kai's love of whimsy and color, as well as their passion for diversity and representation in art, are what inspired them to enter the world of children's literature. In their free time, Kai can be found cuddling cats, collecting stuffed animals, and painting everything rainbow. Rainbow Days is Kai's first early reader series.

YOU Can Draw Zoya!

1 Draw Zoya's head and ear. Start with a circle and draw a cross in the middle of her face.

2 Add two eyes and a nose. Then add eyebrows. (Use the cross you drew in Step 1 to help you place these details!)

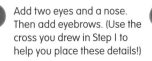

3 Draw Zoya's neck and shoulders. Give her a smile.

4 Draw a large, cloudlike shape on top of her head. Draw a smaller cloud near each shoulder.

5 Draw lines to connect the small clouds to her face. Add details to Zoya's hair. Give her shirt a collar.

6 Color in your drawing!

WHAT'S YOUR STORY?

Zoya loves art! So does her dog, Coco.
Imagine **you** are painting with Zoya and Coco.
What would you paint? What colors would you use?
Would you use glitter?
Write and draw your story!